ALBERT STARTS SCHOOL

by **Eleanor May** • Illustrated by **Deborah Melmon**

THE KANE PRESS / NEW YORK

To Ed Miller, for his creative designs throughout the years
—E.M. and the J's

Acknowledgments: We wish to thank the following people for their helpful advice and review of the material contained in this book: Susan Longo, Early Childhood and Elementary School Teacher, Mamaroneck, NY; and Rebeka Eston Salemi, Kindergarten Teacher, Lincoln School, Lincoln, MA.

Special thanks to Susan Longo for providing the Fun Activities in the back of this book.

Library of Congress Cataloging-in-Publication Data

May, Eleanor.
Albert starts school / by Eleanor May ; illustrated by Deborah Melmon.
pages cm. — (Mouse math)
"With fun activities!"
Summary: On his first day of school, Albert the mouse learns that his favorite activities are scheduled for different days of the week.
ISBN 978-1-57565-741-7 (library reinforced binding : alk. paper) — ISBN 978-1-57565-742-4 (pbk. : alk. paper)
[1. First day of school—Fiction. 2. Schools—Fiction. 3. Days—Fiction. 4. Mice—Fiction.]
I. Melmon, Deborah, illustrator. II. Title.
PZ7.M4513Akr 2015
[E]—dc23
2014038448

eISBN: 978-1-57565-743-1

1 3 5 7 9 10 8 6 4 2

First published in the United States of America in 2015 by Kane Press, Inc.
Printed in the United States of America

Book Design: Edward Miller

Mouse Math is a registered trademark of Kane Press, Inc.

Visit us online at **www.kanepress.com**

 Like us on Facebook
facebook.com/kanepress

 Follow us on Twitter
@KanePress

Dear Parent/Educator,

"I can't do math." Every child (or grownup!) who says these words has at some point along the way felt intimidated by math. For young children who are just being introduced to the subject, we wanted to create a world in which math was not simply numbers on a page, but a part of life—an adventure!

Enter Albert and Wanda, two little mice who live in the walls of a People House. Children will be swept along with this irrepressible duo and their merry band of friends as they tackle mouse-sized problems and dilemmas (and sometimes *cat-sized* problems and dilemmas!).

Each book in the **MOUSE MATH**® series provides a fresh take on a basic math concept. The mice discover solutions as they, for instance, use position words while teaching a pet snail to do tricks or count the alarmingly large number of friends they've invited over on a rainy day—and, lo and behold, they are doing math!

Math educators who specialize in early childhood learning have applied their expertise to make sure each title is as helpful as possible to young children—and to their parents and teachers. Fun activities at the ends of the books and on our website encourage kids to think and talk about math in ways that will make each concept clear and memorable.

As with our award-winning Math Matters® series, our aim is to captivate children's imaginations by drawing them into the story, and so into the math at the heart of each adventure. It is our hope that kids will want to hear and read the **MOUSE MATH** stories again and again and that, as they grow up, they will approach math with enthusiasm and see it as an invaluable tool for navigating the world they live in.

Sincerely,

Joanne Kane

Joanne E. Kane
Publisher

On **Sunday**, Albert could not wait to go to bed.
Tomorrow was his very first day of school!

Sunday	Monday	Tuesday	Wednesday	Thursday	Friday	Saturday

"Does school really have paw painting?"
he asked his sister, Wanda.
"Is there really a piano we can play?
Are you *sure* my teacher will let me feed the class pet?"

Wanda smiled. "Yes, yes, and yes!"

On **Monday**, Wanda dropped off Albert at his classroom.

"Hi, Albert!" said his teacher, Mrs. Munch.
"Welcome to school!"

| Sunday | Monday | Tuesday | Wednesday | Thursday | Friday | Saturday |

"Albert!" Mrs. Munch said a few minutes later.
"What are you doing?"

"I'm getting out the paw paints," Albert said.

"Today is Monday," Mrs. Munch said.
"Tuesday is our art day. We will paint tomorrow."

"Oh," Albert said. "At home I can paint any time I want."

His teacher put a paw around his shoulder.
"Yes. But this is school."

On the way home, Wanda asked Albert,
"How was your first day of school?"

"I didn't get to paint today," he said.

"What *did* you do?" Wanda asked.

"We had story time at the library. With puppets,"
Albert said.

Wanda smiled. "That sounds like fun!"

"It was fun!" Albert said. "But I still want to paint."

The next day was **Tuesday**.

"Art day!" Mrs. Munch announced.

| Sunday | Monday | Tuesday | Wednesday | Thursday | Friday | Saturday |

After painting, Albert went over to the fishbowl.
"Minnie looks hungry," he said. "I'll give her some food."

"Albert! No!" Melody cried.
"Tuesday is my day to feed the fish.
Tomorrow is your turn."

PAW
WASHING

Minnie the Minnow
THIS WEEK'S
FEEDING SCHEDULE

Monday	Leo
Tuesday	Melody
Wednesday	Albert
Thursday	Charlie
Friday	Rachel

"I got to paint today," Albert told Wanda after school.
"But I didn't get to feed our class pet.
At home I get to feed my pet every day."

Wanda said, "School isn't the same as home.
But it's fun, too."

The next day was **Wednesday**.
Albert beamed. "My turn to feed the fish!"

Albert fed Minnie. Then he went to the piano.

Minnie the Minnow
THIS WEEK'S
FEEDING SCHEDULE

Monday	Leo
Tuesday	Melody
Wednesday	Albert
Thursday	Charlie
Friday	Rachel

Hi, Minnie!

| Sunday | Monday | Tuesday | Wednesday | Thursday | Friday | Saturday |

15

"Albert!" Mrs. Munch said. "What are you doing?"

"Playing the piano," Albert said. "Today is music day!"

Mrs. Munch said, "But it's nap time now."

"At home I only nap when I feel tired," Albert said.

Mrs. Munch sighed.

"I know," Albert said. "This is school."

Thursday was gym day.
Albert's class played Cat Attack and Flying Cheese.

When their teacher came to pick them up,
Albert said, "Do we have to go so soon? At home—"

Mrs. Munch crossed her paws. "Yes, Albert?"

| Sunday | Monday | Tuesday | Wednesday | **Thursday** | Friday | Saturday |

19

Albert smiled.

"At home we NEVER get to play these games!"

On **Friday**, Mrs. Munch had a surprise.
"We have a new student!" she told the class.
"This is Frankie.
Who would like to show Frankie around?"

Albert's paw shot up.

| Sunday | Monday | Tuesday | Wednesday | Thursday | Friday | Saturday |

Albert showed Frankie the fishbowl.
"This is Minnie," Albert said. "She's our class pet."

"Can I feed her?" Frankie asked.

PAW
WASHING

Minnie the Minnow
THIS WEEK'S
FEEDING SCHEDULE

Monday	Leo
Tuesday	Melody
Wednesday	Albert
Thursday	Charlie
Friday	Rachel

"You'll get a turn next week," Albert explained.
"Today is Friday, so it's Rachel's turn.
Charlie fed her yesterday, and my turn was the day before."

"We do something special every day," Albert said.
"Monday is library. Tuesday is art. Wednesday is music.
Thursday is gym. And today we make our own class snack!"

MONDAY

TUESDAY

WEDNESDAY

THURSDAY

"Sometimes I help make snacks at home," Frankie said.

"Me too," Albert said. "But this is different. . . ."

25

"This is school!"

"There's a new mouse in our class!"
Albert told Wanda after school.
"Tomorrow I'm going to play with him at recess."

"But Albert, tomorrow is **Saturday**," Wanda said.
"On Saturday there isn't any school."

"No school?" Albert's face fell.

Sunday	Monday	Tuesday	Wednesday	Thursday	Friday	Saturday

"At home you can do anything you like," Wanda reminded him. "You can read or rest or paint or play—any time."

Albert perked up. "That's right! I can! And you know what I'm going to do first?"

"I'm going to play SCHOOL!"

FUN ACTIVITIES ❸ 4

Albert Starts School supports children's understanding of **days of the week** and their correct sequential order. Use the activities below to extend this early math learning topic and to support children's early reading skills.

🐭 ENGAGE

Remind children that the cover of a book as well as the title can tell them a lot about the story inside.

▶ Before reading the story, have children look at the cover as you read the title. Ask: *Where do you think this story takes place? What do you think this story is about?*

▶ Ask children about activities they do at school during the week.

▶ Ask: *Did you know what things you would do at school before you actually started school?* (Some children might have heard from older brothers or sisters about what to expect.)

▶ Now read the story to find out what fun new activities Albert gets to do in his school and on which days of the week he does them.

🐭 LOOK BACK

▶ After reading the story, ask: *Do you think Albert was excited about going to school? What makes you think so?*

▶ Ask: *What different activities did Albert do in school?*

▶ Ask: *Did Albert know there was a weekly schedule that he was supposed to follow? Who told him about the schedule?*

▶ Ask: *What did the weekly schedule tell Albert?* Help children recall that the schedule gave the days of the week in their correct order and listed the activities for each day.

▶ Referring to the story, re-create Albert's classroom schedule on a piece of easel paper or on a whiteboard if one is available. List the five weekdays, starting with **Monday**, followed by the activity for each day.

▶ Read the list aloud in unison.

MONDAY · Library
TUESDAY · Art
WEDNESDAY · Music
THURSDAY · Gym
FRIDAY · Snacks

🐭 TRY THIS!

On a large sheet of paper or on flashcards, write the names of the seven days of the week, Monday through Sunday. Then review the meanings of the words *today*, *yesterday*, and *tomorrow*.

Tell children that they are going to take turns being the teacher in a classroom and asking questions about days of the week. Point out that they are going to use the names of the days of the week and the words *today*, *yesterday*, and *tomorrow*.

▶ Model the activity by pointing to a day of the week (Monday through Friday because children are pretending to be in school) and say, "**Today** is (day of week you point to)."

▶ Then ask, "What day of the week was it **yesterday**?" and "What day will it be **tomorrow**?" Have children name the days of the week that answer the questions, and check that everyone understands the activity.

▶ Then have children take turns being the teacher by following the procedure and asking the questions you modeled for them.

🐭 THINK!

Provide crayons, pencils, and a stapler. Have available several sheets of paper for each child. (The number of sheets will depend on how large the children write, how they finish each sentence, and their drawings.)

▶ Begin by writing or by having children write the following sentence starter: On Monday, I like to _____.

▶ Have children complete the sentence. After the sentence, children may draw a picture to illustrate what they like to do.

▶ Using a similar sentence starter, have children repeat the procedure for the rest of the days of the week through Sunday.

▶ When children have finished, they may staple the sheets of paper together to make a **Days of the Week** booklet.

▶ When everyone is done, children can share their booklets.

◆ **FOR MORE ACTIVITIES** ◆
visit www.kanepress.com/mouse-math-activities